T0115515

ACKNOWLEDGMENT

The quotes in the text are from the 1896 and 1906 editions of the
Boston Cooking School Cookbook by Fannie Merritt Farmer, except
for a slight adjustment in the griddle cakes recipe.

First Aladdin Paperbacks edition August 2004

Text copyright © 2001 by Deborah Hopkinson
Illustrations copyright © 2001 by Nancy Carpenter

ALADDIN PAPERBACKS
An imprint of Simon & Schuster
Children's Publishing Division
1230 Avenue of the Americas
New York, NY 10020

All rights reserved, including the right of
reproduction in whole or in part in any form.

Also available in an Atheneum Books for Young Readers
hardcover edition.
Designed by Lee Wade
The text of this book was set in Celestia Antiqua.

Manufactured in China
12 13 14 15 16 17 18 19 20

The Library of Congress has cataloged the hardcover edition as follows:
Hopkinson, Deborah.
Fannie in the kitchen / by Deborah Hopkinson ; illustrated by Nancy
Carpenter. — 1st ed. p. cm.
"The whole story from soup to nuts of how Fannie Farmer invented
recipes with precise measurements, including helpful hints from her
famous cookbook."
"An Anne Schwartz book."
Summary: Fannie Farmer is a mother's helper in the Shaw house, where
the daughter gives her the idea of writing down precise instructions for
measuring and cooking, which eventually became one of the first
modern cookbooks.
ISBN 978-0-689-81965-4
1. Cookery—Juvenile literature. 2. Farmer, Fannie Merritt, 1857-1915—
Juvenile literature.
[1. Farmer, Fannie, 1857-1915. 2. Cookery.]
I. Carpenter, Nancy, ill. II. Title.
TX652.5.H62 1999
641.5—dc21 97-46712
CIP AC

ISBN 978-0-689-86997-6 (pbk.)

0921 SCP

To Vicki, with love and thanks for many
years of friendship, and many wonderful
meals! — DH

To Gene — NC

Including
Helpful Hints
from Her
Famous Cookbook

FANNIE IN THE KITCHEN

The Whole Story from Soup to Nuts of How
Fannie Farmer Invented Recipes with Precise Measurements

by DEBORAH HOPKINSON
pictures by NANCY CARPENTER

ALADDIN PAPERBACKS
NEW YORK LONDON TORONTO SYDNEY

First Course (the Soup)
We Meet Marcia

Marcia Shaw could do many things extremely well. She could make long perfect candles,

scrub clothes on the washboard until they were spotless,

and polish the oil lamps till they shined.

Mama is lucky to have a helper like me, Marcia decided.

But one day Mama announced, "A girl named Fannie Farmer is coming here to live. She'll be my mother's helper."

"What about me?" asked Marcia. "*I'm* your helper."

"Yes, dear," said Mama. "But with Baby coming I need someone to cook."

Marcia scowled at Mama's big fancy stove. She didn't want a new baby. Or a girl named Fannie. She could only hope Fannie Farmer didn't know how to cook.

SECOND COURSE
A *Small Success*

But from the very first morning Fannie arrived, it was clear she *did* know how to cook.

"What delicious eggs," Mama said at breakfast.

Papa chewed happily. "And these biscuits. So light and flaky!"

Marcia folded her arms. *I won't eat,* she decided. *Then they'll be sorry they brought her here.*

Papa reached over and plucked a biscuit off her plate. "Marcia, would you please ask Fannie if there are any more?"

FANNIE'S HINT

Biscuits should
always be small …
Large biscuits,
though equally
good, never
tempt one by
their daintiness.

As Marcia pushed open the kitchen door, toasty-warm smells tickled her nose.

"Papa wants more biscuits," she said rudely.

"Coming up," Fannie replied pleasantly.

Fannie plunked a wooden spoon into Marcia's hand.

"You can help. Just spoon the dough onto the pan while I check the fire."

"Make them nice and small," Fannie added. "Small biscuits are more dainty, don't you think?"

Marcia stood still. Why should she help? Still, it did look rather fun.

Later, when Marcia brought out her basket of steaming biscuits, she couldn't resist saying, "I made them."

After breakfast, Marcia snuck a biscuit and popped it into her mouth.

It was small, light, and flaky. Just delicious.

THIRD COURSE
The Griddle Cake Mistake

Fannie was making griddle cakes, golden brown and steaming hot, as Marcia watched. "The biggest mistake with griddle cakes," said Fannie, waving her turner, "is to flip them at the wrong time."

"When is the right time?" asked Marcia.

"Look at this one," Fannie instructed. "Is it puffed?"

Marcia looked closely. "It's puffed."

"Is it full of bubbles?"

Marcia nodded. Little bubbles were popping up all over.

"Then now is precisely the right time." With one sweep Fannie flipped the cake in the air and neatly back onto the griddle.

FANNIE'S HINT

♦ ♦ ♦

Drop batter by spoonfuls on a greased hot griddle; cook on one side. When puffed, full of bubbles and cooked on edges, turn, and cook other side. Serve with butter and maple syrup.

"Let me try." Marcia grabbed the turner. "I don't need help, I was watching."

Fannie raised an eyebrow. "Fine, I'll have a cup of tea."

Marcia clutched the turner. She checked to see if Fannie was looking. But Fannie was curled up with the newspaper, cozy as the cat at her feet.

Marcia flipped the first cake too early. It came out mushy in the middle.

She flipped the second cake too late. It was already completely black on the edges.

Then Marcia flipped the third griddle cake—just when it was puffed and full of bubbles.

She flipped it right onto the cat.

"Well, you did flip it at the right time," Fannie said. "Precisely the right time."

FOURTH COURSE
The Egg Disaster

When Baby was born, Marcia wanted to bake a special cake for Mama—all by herself. After all, how hard could it be?

Marcia put on Fannie's best apron. She measured flour, then beat the butter and sugar till they were light and fluffy.

I'm baking a cake! I can do this extremely well, she said to herself.

But when Marcia cracked the first egg into the bowl, pieces of shell fell into the batter. Even more shell dropped in when she cracked the second egg. And on the third, the most awful, the most horrid, the most odious smell filled the kitchen.

Fannie walked in and grabbed her nose. "Ooh, a rotten egg!"

Marcia looked at her ruined cake. Tears filled her eyes.

FANNIE'S HINT
◆ ◆ ◆
The mixing and baking of cake requires more care and judgment than any other branch of cookery. . . .

But Fannie just waved a hand in the air. "Everyone finds rotten eggs sometimes. Next time, try this." She held up an egg. "First, hold it in front of a candle flame in a dark room; the center should look clear."

"Second, place it in a basin of cold water; it should sink."

"Third, place the large end to your cheek; a warmth should be felt."

And so Marcia learned the three ways to determine the freshness of eggs. "Thank you, Fannie," she said. "Now, could you help me bake a cake?"

FIFTH COURSE
An Excellent Idea

After Baby came, all Mama wanted to do was play with him. Marcia found this disgusting, so she began to spend more time with Fannie in the kitchen.

Marcia liked the kitchen. Mysterious spices scented the air, and copper pans gleamed above her head like autumn moons.

And Marcia decided that, after all, she liked Fannie. Fannie seemed like a magician who could make mashed potatoes fluffier than clouds and blueberry pies sweeter than a summer sky.

FANNIE'S HINT
◆ ◆ ◆
Correct measurements are
absolutely necessary to insure
the best results.

"Cookery is magic," declared Marcia one day, crunching a hot gingersnap.

Fannie shook her head. "Preparing food well isn't magic. It's an art and a science that anyone can learn."

"Anyone but me," Marcia grumbled. "There's too much to remember. At least *you* have it all in your head."

"I do have a lot in my head," Fannie said thoughtfully. "But Marcia, what if I wrote out precise instructions for you? Then you could cook exactly as I do."

"Will you explain *everything*?" asked Marcia excitedly. "How to mix a fancy cake, make a pot of soup, even measure a cup of flour?"

"Everything," Fannie promised.

Fannie got a huge notebook and began right away.

She explained how to
measure a spoonful of
salt so that it's exactly level,

and how to choose the ripest
melons in the market.

She even wrote directions for the three ways
to determine the freshness of eggs.

Word of Fannie's notebook began to spread. Marcia's mother consulted it to make the special sauce Papa loved so much. Neighbors dropped in to borrow this recipe or that, or to ask Fannie's advice.

Best of all, the notebook made cooking much easier for Marcia.

"Fannie, if I can learn to cook using your book, anyone can," Marcia said. "Why, I believe you could teach the whole town of Boston to cook."

"What an excellent idea," said Fannie. "Maybe I'll try."

SIXTH COURSE
Marcia Shaw, Master Chef

And so Fannie decided to become a cooking teacher at the Boston Cooking School. Marcia was sad to see her go, but she was sure Fannie would be the best teacher there.

Before Fannie left, Marcia wanted to bake her a special cake. She knew just what to do.

FANNIE'S HINT

◆ ◆ ◆

Before attempting to mix cake, study *How to Measure* and *How to Combine Ingredients.*

In Fannie's cookery notebook, Marcia found the recipe for Golden Cake.

She read it carefully; she measured, mixed, and combined.

Then she put the cake in the oven and baked it just until it was done.

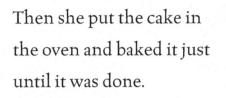

"You made this by yourself?" asked Mama in surprise.

"So tasty," Papa said with his mouth full. Even Baby got a big piece.

Fannie took a bite and chewed slowly. Marcia held her breath.

"Marcia Shaw, you can do many things extremely well," Fannie announced at last. "You can bake small, dainty biscuits, always spot a rotten egg, and flip griddle cakes at precisely the right time."

Fannie paused. "You can also bake an excellent cake."

Marcia laughed and picked up her fork. She took a bite of cake.

Just delicious.

SEVENTH COURSE (THE NUTS)
More About Fannie Farmer

Some people say Fannie Merritt Farmer invented the modern recipe. She was one of the first to publish a book with exact instructions for measuring and cooking. Fannie's *Boston Cooking School Cookbook* (often called *The Fannie Farmer Cookbook*) is over one hundred years old, but it's so popular people still know and use it.

Less is known about the real Fannie. She was born in Boston, Massachusetts, in 1857. At about age sixteen she became ill with polio or had a mild stroke that left her with a limp in her left leg. Fannie became a mother's helper in the home of Mr. and Mrs. Charles Shaw. It seems it was there, while teaching young Marcia, that Fannie realized how much easier cooking would be if ingredients were measured precisely for every recipe.

Fannie went on to be a teacher at the Boston Cooking School and later was named its principal. After her cookbook was published in 1896 she became known all over the country. Throughout her life, Fannie had a special interest in teaching people about nutrition and health. She died in 1915.

Remember, if you follow Fannie's instructions exactly, you can make griddle cakes (we call them pancakes now) for your whole family. And you will know how to flip them at precisely the right time.

Fannie Farmer's Famous Griddle Cakes

2 cups flour

¼ cup sugar

1 tsp salt

1 ½ tbs baking powder

1 egg

2 cups milk

2 tbs melted butter

Mix and sift dry ingredients; beat egg, add milk, and pour slowly on first mixture. Beat thoroughly and add butter. Drop by spoonfuls on a greased hot griddle; cook on one side. When puffed, full of bubbles, and cooked on edges, turn and cook other side.

Serve with butter and maple syrup.

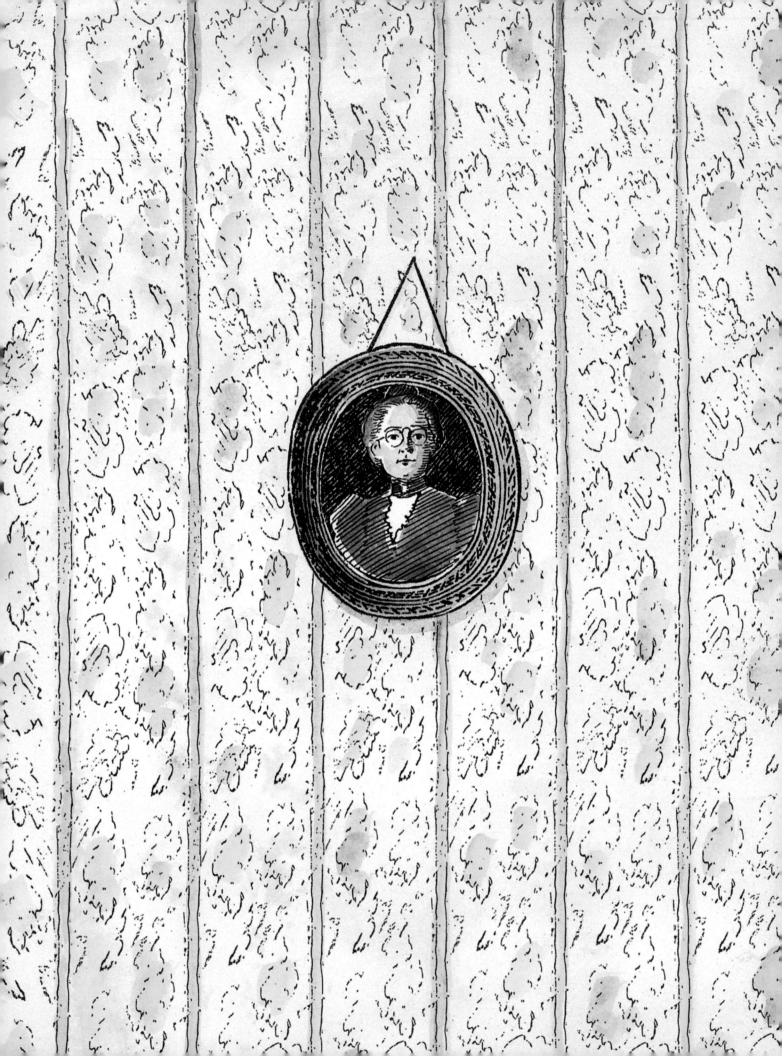